Duck
on holiday

Notes for Parents

This is a book to share with a young child who is beginning to talk. At this stage of their development, children need lots of opportunities to learn new words and phrases, and lots of practice using those they already know in different ways and situations. Each picture in this book is designed to stimulate discussion about what Duck is doing and about the things around him. There are objects to name and things to spot or count. The text on each page is intended only as a starting point for wider conversation.

Very young children have to learn that a book has a sequence and that, by starting at the beginning and turning the pages one by one, they can follow this sequence to find out what happens next. The pictures in this book tell a short, very simple story for children who are just ready to learn this important new skill.

Duck
on holiday

Jenny Tyler and Philip Hawthorn
Illustrated by Stephen Cartwright

Consultant: Betty Root
Edited by Heather Amery

Here's Duck who thinks, this sunny day,
The beach is just the place to play.

This nice cool rock pool seems to be
The perfect Duck-sized bit of sea.

He steers his rubber ring with style,
And chats to Fish for quite a while.

Then sails his yacht, and calls with glee,
"Ahoy there, shipmates, look at me!"

Duck slurps a drink, gets nicely tanned,
And eats a sandwich on the sand.

This nice cool rock pool seems to be
The perfect Duck-sized bit of sea.

He steers his rubber ring with style,
And chats to Fish for quite a while.

Then sails his yacht, and calls with glee,
"Ahoy there, shipmates, look at me!"

Duck slurps a drink, gets nicely tanned,
And eats a sandwich on the sand.

He builds a castle, digs a moat,
Adds flags and shells, and then his boat.

The ball goes smash, poor Duck starts crying,
Shells go crash, and flags go flying.

Dog shares his nice ice cream with Duck,
To make up for his rotten luck.

The two new friends then scream and shout,
While whizzing round and round about.

It's time to go, Duck feels so sad,
He thinks of all the fun he's had.

It's hard to leave, but have no fear,
He'll see his friends again next year.

First published in 1987. This enlarged edition first published in 1992. Usborne Publishing Ltd. Usborne House, 83-85 Saffron Hill, London ECIN 8RT. Copyright © Usborne Publishing Ltd. 1992

First published in America August 1995.